This book is dedicated to anyone who reads it or just enjoyed the pictures.
I hope you grab this world with both hands and doubters be gone.
Don't forget, it's never too late to have a happy childhood my brothers and sisters.
To my very funny husband, thanks for the laughter and never saying "no," because I hate "no" and "yes" is so much more fun and to my sweet daughter, you're beyond beautiful in all the ways that truly count.
Stay cool kitty.

Text and illustrations © 2022 Emma Lamport
Art direction and design: Caroline Grimshaw
Printed and bound in Wales by Gomer Press Ltd.

thegiftemmalamport.com

The Gift

Perin and
the Nautilus

STORY AND ILLUSTRATIONS
BY EMMA LAMPORT

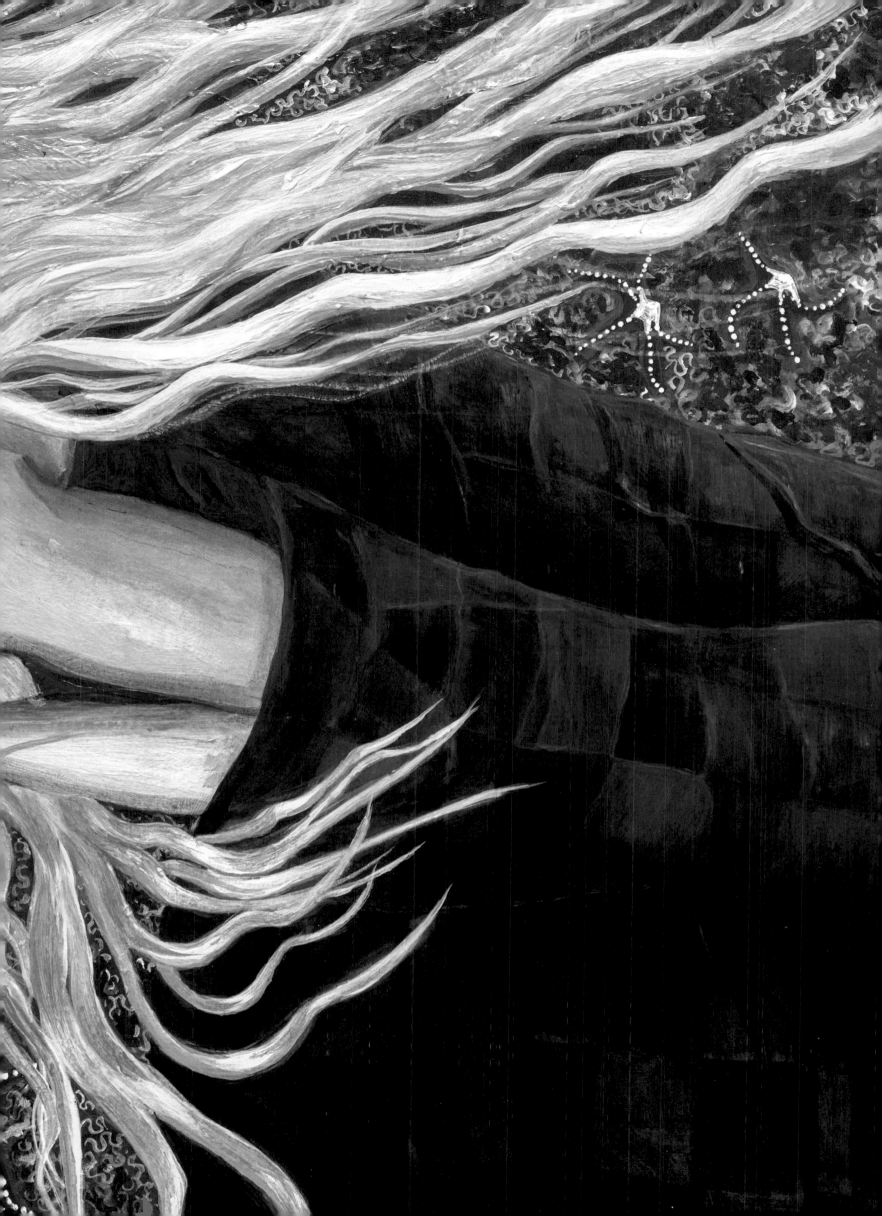

On a perfect day like all others, Perin awoke to the familiar pull of her kelp-woven blanket.

As the tide changed, and began to withdraw, it tugged away the velvety, seaweed cloth — exposing the tip of her shimmering, silvery tail, which twitched as soon as it became uncovered.

Perin opened one eye, and delighted in watching her tail smack gently against the cold, smooth rocks of her bed.

Before she had the chance to stretch, a friendly face appeared in the opening of her small but perfect cave.

It was Haze, a young seal pup. He was much like Perin: equally as curious, fun-loving, and endlessly energetic. He had the enthusiasm of an entire school of dolphins, all wrapped up into one rather adorable-looking, spotted grey seal pup. He lived closer to humans than Perin did, at the end of an abandoned pier in a nearby harbour.

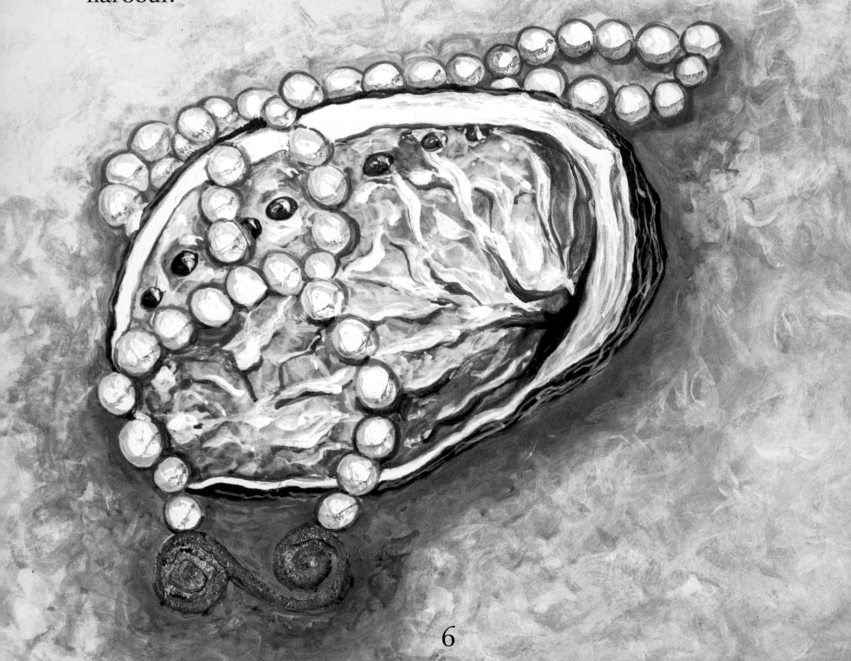

"Wake up Perin, I've spotted a human boy at Swan Cove," he said.

"What's he doing?" Perin asked, instantly bright-eyed. Quickly pulling back her kelp blanket, she reached for her precious pearl necklace.

"He's got a net and is carrying fins."

"Whose fins?" exclaimed Perin, alarmed by how a human boy could be holding a sea creature's fins.

"I don't know," said Haze, "but he's got a pair of them and a mask!"

Perin grabbed her pre-made sea cucumber sandwich, and the pair darted out of the cave.

They travelled through her manicured kelp garden, slalomed through the bull kelp, and around mountains of spiky, red and purple sea urchins (who were all chattering loudly as they munched their way through their sea greens).

Then the pair swam along the sandy ocean floor, and past the carpet of perfectly camouflaged Starry Flounders, who peered up at them, blinking.

Finally, Perin and Haze swam into the shallow waters of the inner reef, and up into the safety of a floating island of Turkish towel seaweed.

"Good Morning Mr. Otter," said Haze, politely.

"Morning seal pup," said Otto the Otter, not looking at them but continuing to float on his back, trying to crack open a scallop he'd caught earlier by hitting it with his favourite beach stone.

Perin and Haze carefully slid out of the water, making sure not to make a sound or any ripples, and took watch from behind a little group of pinnacles.

Sure enough, walking on the craggy shore was a small human boy. His skin was sun-kissed and his hair was blond and quite long; it almost covered his piercing blue eyes, which Perin was delighted to see were the colour of the Pacific Ocean.

He sat down and laid out his things: two stiff fins, a mask and snorkel, as well as a long, blunt metal object and a small net.

Perin and Haze looked on eagerly.

"What's he doing?" Haze said quietly to Perin.

"I have no idea," Perin replied, her eyes following the boy's every move, entranced.

Curious, they both watched as he gazed out to sea. He seemed to be in deep thought, concentrating on the patterns of the waves as they rolled in and out.

"Look," said Haze, continuing to whisper, "he knows how to study wave patterns."

The pair listened closely as the boy counted out loud how long it took for the next set of waves to break on the shore.

"This boy might be cleverer than the others," Haze said.

"Yes, and look, he's wearing The Symbol around his neck. It only has one spiral, though. I wonder where the other went," said Perin, stroking her own precious necklace. She was further enchanted and somewhat puzzled.

After some time, the boy got up. He calmly put on his mask, then his snorkel, and he put the metal tool into his shorts. Adjusting his mask, he went down to the water's edge, and slipped on his fins as the little waves lapped around his ankles. Each action seemed carefully planned out as though he were performing a ritual. Lastly, the boy picked up his net, and within a moment he had dived in and under the rolling waves.

"Oh my," Haze said, flipping and flapping in a dither, "he's coming towards us!"

"Yes, but he hasn't seen us!" Perin pointed out, and the pair dove down. Cautiously, they sheltered once more out of sight, behind the base of the giant pinnacles.

Perin and Haze watched the boy swim above them. With his cheeks puffed out, he attempted to hold his breath as he dove quickly to the ocean floor, kicking vigorously: ten, twenty, thirty feet down, before reaching the bottom. He then instantly began searching for something — pulling at the roots of the bull kelp and picking up rocks, looking in the cracks and crevices. Finally, with one sudden, giant kick, he turned and thrust himself upwards to the water's surface, gulping in a mighty breath of air.

"Oh dear," Haze said, dismayed, "he's not much of a swimmer, is he?"

"Oh, but he is, said Perin, sympathetically. "He just can't hold his breath for very long. After all, he's a human boy, not a fish or a seabird or a seal."

"Is he fishing or swimming or playing hide and seek?" Haze asked excitedly but still rather confused.

"He's looking for something, and you're going to help him find it!"

Smiling broadly, Perin pointed back to the kelp forest, her bright and watery eyes now twinkling with delight.

"Oh, turban snails! I hoped you were going to say that, because I'm an excellent finder," Haze said, doing loops at high speed around the mermaid. Then, in an exuberant froth of bubbles, the seal pup swam up to the water's surface.

When Haze reached the boy, he began telling him he knew where to find the treasure he was seeking. "It's abalone, isn't it? I know it's abalone! It is, it is! I can help. Oh, this is outstanding, isn't it?" the seal pup exclaimed in a trill of loud squeaks and fish-scented barks, performing such giant leaps in the air that the boy was soaked under a rainstorm of seawater.

He's not following me down, Haze thought to himself. That's surprising. Thinking the boy was maybe hard of hearing, he continued to bark, but this time even louder.

But no! It seemed clear that, although the boy was surprisingly unafraid of the playful pup, he didn't understand a word of "SEAL" he was saying…

So, Haze decided to try and talk the universal language of the sea: that of actions. After all, he thought, the octopus sprays ink as a warning to keep away; dolphins leap in great schools, in order to explain the hunt is beginning and to locate other pods; and leopard sharks go head first into holes, exposing just their tails, to let it be known they're sleeping... And everyone understands that!

Haze stopped barking and slowed his movements. He circled the boy at a slight distance, not splashing, and motioned with his flippers, ducking under the water again and again.

This time, the boy followed.

As the pair reached the bottom, Haze began parting the curtains of bull kelp with his nose. At once, an entire hidden wall of prized abalone was revealed. Most were over ten inches in size, and there were dozens of these giant molluscs!

The boy quickly pulled out his long and flat metal tool, prying an abalone off the rocks, before putting it in his small net. He then extracted another two. He nodded to the seal slowly in a gesture of great thanks, and kicked hard back up to the water's surface.

Haze waited but the boy did not return. He was puzzled yet again by the nature and actions of this small human. As he pondered, he could see Perin through the kelp. She was beckoning him over to their hiding spot, and the young seal quickly rejoined the mermaid.

Perin looked greatly pleased.

"You have done well, my friend. Thank you." She stretched out her arms, bowing her head a little, and blinked in unison with the seal. "I am also very impressed with this young human boy. He has followed the ocean code by only taking what he can eat. He seems ungoverned by greed, which is very rare. He is very special, and so we will reward him once more. I have another great task for you Haze; this one is very important. You must go and find Homer, the ancient sea turtle."

"Why?" Haze asked, inquisitively.

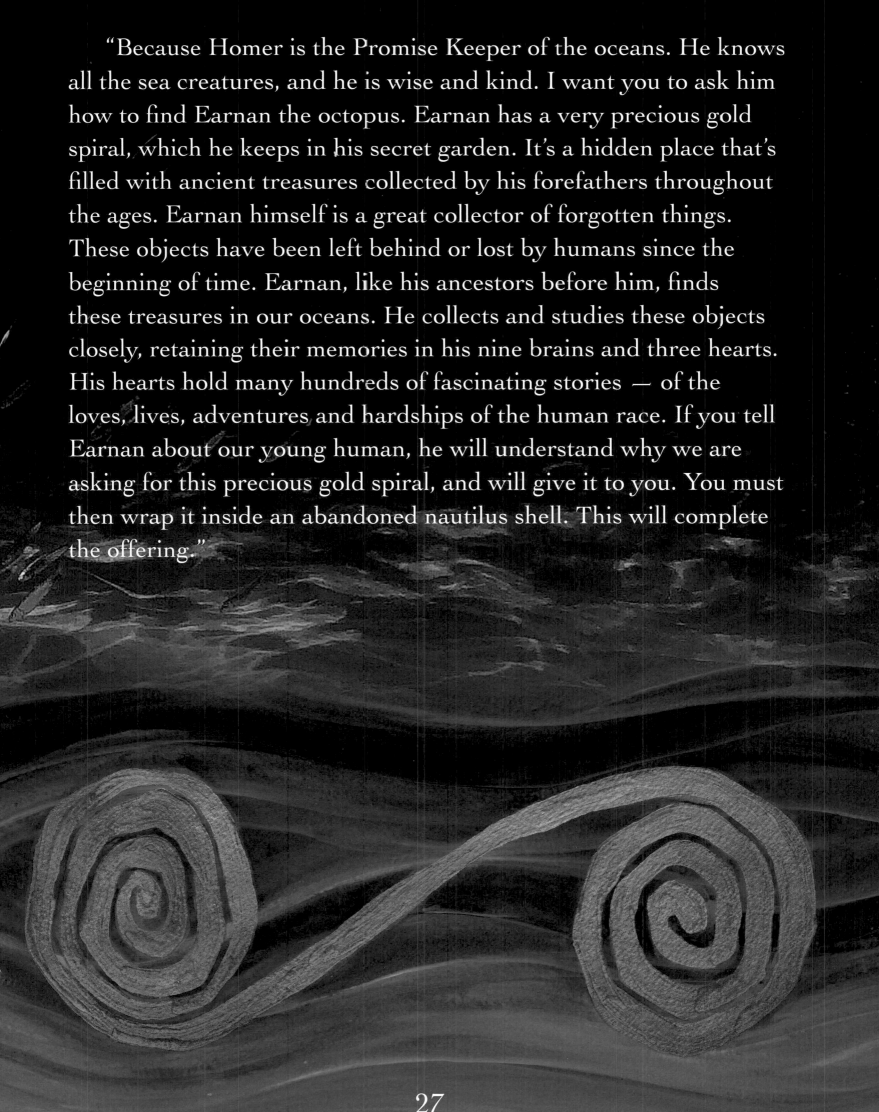

"Because Homer is the Promise Keeper of the oceans. He knows all the sea creatures, and he is wise and kind. I want you to ask him how to find Earnan the octopus. Earnan has a very precious gold spiral, which he keeps in his secret garden. It's a hidden place that's filled with ancient treasures collected by his forefathers throughout the ages. Earnan himself is a great collector of forgotten things. These objects have been left behind or lost by humans since the beginning of time. Earnan, like his ancestors before him, finds these treasures in our oceans. He collects and studies these objects closely, retaining their memories in his nine brains and three hearts. His hearts hold many hundreds of fascinating stories — of the loves, lives, adventures and hardships of the human race. If you tell Earnan about our young human, he will understand why we are asking for this precious gold spiral, and will give it to you. You must then wrap it inside an abandoned nautilus shell. This will complete the offering."

With great swiftness, the harbour seal Haze swam out of the safety of the inner reef, dropping down into far deeper waters.

Soon enough, he found Homer the sea turtle, who was slowly and gracefully gliding by.

"Respectfully, Mr. Homer, can you help me find Earnan the octopus?"

"I'm not one to give out another sea creature's location, young pup," Homer said cautiously, "but I can see you mean him no harm, so I will help you. Please respect the secrecy of his dwelling place, and safe travels!"

With Homer's instructions, the seal darted off once more; the thrill of adventure was in his mind and honour in his heart. Not many seal pups had ever met the highly elusive Earnan the octopus.

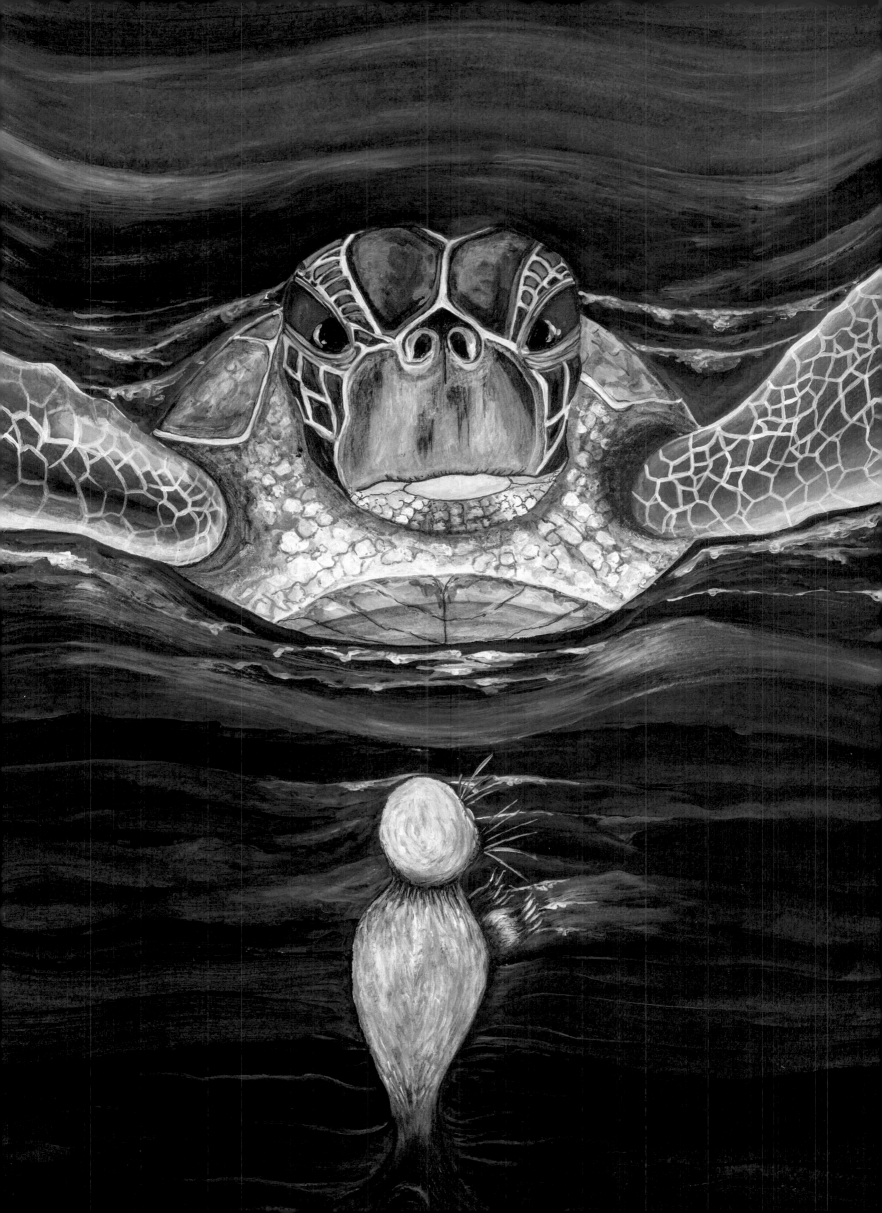

Haze picked up his pace, as these were dangerous, uncharted waters for a young seal far from his home in the harbour. He went through cathedral rock canyons, passing schools of skipjack tuna, and then headed further down into a rather eerie-looking cave opening.

Sure enough, even in the near darkness, he could make out the twinkling of a few dancing lights. He followed the mere glints deep into the cavern. Suddenly, as the cave entrance became smaller, a great mass of tentacles came out through the gloom.

"Who goes there?" the creature demanded.

"Haze the seal! Perin the mermaid and Homer the turtle sent me to find you," the rather alarmed little pup exclaimed.

"Then you may enter." There was a pause before the tentacles withdrew, revealing a small entrance to an expansive cavern beyond. "I am Earnan the Knowing. Welcome to my garden."

Haze slowly made his way inside. His already giant eyes widened even further in amazement at the bejewelled cave. It was filled with objects made from precious metals, heaps of gemstones in all the colours of a kaleidoscope, and various anchors of all shapes and sizes, as well as a beautifully carved human woman that once would have adorned the bowsprit of a great ship.

The seal was entranced for a moment but then drew his gaze back to the enormous octopus, who took up most of the space. He blinked in welcome, and continued to explain his quest while Earnan listened.

When Haze had finished, Earnan agreed to help, and gifted the seal pup the ancient gold spiral.

"This was said to have come from a forgotten shipwreck off the coast of South America," the giant octopus said. "However, I have other examples of the symbol from all around the Americas and as far as the Irish Sea and the Scottish coastline."

Earnan explained the object's wisdom, and how the spiral represented many things —including the circle of life, embodying birth and rebirth, as well as the values of taking, giving and receiving, and the importance of ensuring these were always kept in balance.

The octopus continued, telling stories of humans from long ago, and about the many types of people from around the oceans; how they are bonded with all of life. He explained how for centuries those humans who lived good lives understood the symbol, and tried to maintain harmony. He showed numerous other treasures that symbolised similar balance, and the seal listened intently to the wise octopus.

Earnan then grasped hold of the gold spiral with his large but sensitive tentacles, slipping it into a beautiful nautilus shell that had been left empty, and rolling it around until it made its way safely to the centre.

"This nautilus is a reminder to our ocean kind of eternal life. It is a humble creature but is housed in this magnificent and greatly symbolic shell. It, too, spirals around like life ever after. It reminds us that we must treasure our ocean, and respect its codes."

With those wise words, Haze thanked the octopus for his gift and his inspiring insight, then once more made haste.

With the nautilus shell clenched firmly in his jaw, Haze returned to the safety of the inner reef. As he approached the shoreline, he began slapping the water, trying to get the boy's attention.

The small human was now sat on the shore. His few things and the abalone were bundled up neatly in his net. Sensing the commotion, he turned instantly.

"Hey pup, whatcha got there?" the boy asked, smiling at the seal, believing Haze could understand his every word. Skipping a few paces down to the water's edge, the boy knelt down in the sea foam. "What a magnificent shell!" he exclaimed.

Haze blinked slowly, then neatly released the offering from his jaw. At the exact same time, the boy stretched his hands wide, catching the shell — and out slid the golden spiral. It lay in the wet sand, glistening up at him, and he gazed at it in disbelief, not knowing if he should pick it up.

"Wow, look at that! That's incredible," the boy said, voicing his thoughts out loud.

The seal slapped the water one last time, dousing the boy in a final briny spray, and then he was gone, back into the ocean.

The boy sat in the sand, looking out towards the horizon, and daydreaming about all that had happened that day. The sun was still warm enough to gently bathe his skin and dry his wet, salty hair. He breathed in every last second that the sun had left to offer. He knew shortly it would set behind the ocean's deep curtain, and this magical day would come to an end.

He looked once more at the waves; they were now wide and slow as they limped their way to the shore with barely enough momentum to even break. He felt exactly the same: exhausted but utterly content. He had enjoyed the tests the ocean had given him, and he breathed out great thanks to its width and breadth. He felt such gratitude for the extraordinary gifts he'd been given; he was at peace, despite making no sense of it all.

These thoughts gave him a great calmness, which washed over him and flushed his heart with joy.

It was only after many minutes of daydreaming, and looking out towards the horizon, that the boy noticed he'd been running his fingers around the smooth contours and circles of the nautilus shell. Finally, he looked down and examined it properly. Its clean and brilliant white background was adorned with chestnut brown patterns that decreased in size as they moved inwards towards the centre of the spiral.

Looking under the shell at the sand beneath, he saw the brilliant gold charm cushioned there. Now, he picked it up. Raising it to his eye level, he inspected it closely, and was instantly surprised by its utter perfection. Lacking neither shine nor lustre, it was untarnished — and yet was obviously very old, possibly ancient.

The boy looked closer still, and could make out hundreds of tiny indentations where an artist's hammer had once worked the precious gold metal into its present form. He was reminded of artefacts he'd once seen in a museum. Now he clasped a real treasure of his very own. He wondered about its age, its history and its origin, and who may have owned it before.

The boy untied the leather cord around his neck, and linked his own spiral pendant to its new twin brother. Then, he retied it with a sliding knot, and there it was: the old and the new, around his neck as if they'd always been together.

What are the chances of having two spirals, he thought laughing out loud.

Standing, the boy picked up his net, which had his belongings bound inside. With the last of his energy, he slung it over one shoulder, heaving a little under its weight as the mesh dug into his bare skin.

He turned one last time to the ocean, sea foam still frothing around his toes, and he took in a deep, final breath of mineralised, salty air. He held it in, then closed his eyes — and exhaled. Opening them again, he shouted out with all his might: "My name is Flavian Earwyn! And I am your friend!"

With that, the boy turned and disappeared back over the dunes, heading off into the distance.

The End

GLOSSARY

HARBOR SEALS are found along the northern Hemisphere from the Atlantic to the Pacific Ocean. They can live up to 35 years and weigh up to 370 lbs. They like to forage in shallow water; they are solitary and every individual has unique patterns and spots.

RED ABALONE are Marine Gastropod Molluscs found between British Columbia Canada to Baja Mexico. They live in rocky areas of kelp and enjoy a seaweed diet. They can live from the intertidal zone down to 600 ft.

RED SEA URCHINS' colours vary from pink, red to deep purple. They are found in the north eastern Pacific Ocean from Alaska to Baja Mexico. They can live in shallow water down to 900 ft and like to feed on a diet of seaweed.

STARRY FLOUNDER will swim around like normal fish when young, but soon begin to tilt over to one side and eventually live lying on the sandy sea floor. They live as far south as Japan and Korea and over to Alaska, Canada, and down to the South of California in the USA.

SEA CUCUMBER are marine animals found on the sea floor worldwide, with greater numbers found in Pacific Asia. They help recycle nutrients and generally grow to 4-12 inches in length. They mostly eat Algae and tiny floating particles.

SKIPJACK TUNA grow up to 3 ft in length and prefer warmer waters. They are fast swimming, streamlined pelagic fish found throughout the world. They travel in schools of up to 50,000 fish, feeding on crustaceans, cephalopods and molluscs.

TURKISH TOWEL SEAWEED is greenish in ultraviolet light, but can go from dark red to purple in colour. It can grow fast in the summer months, slower in winter and is found on the Pacific Coast of North America. It's edible to humans.